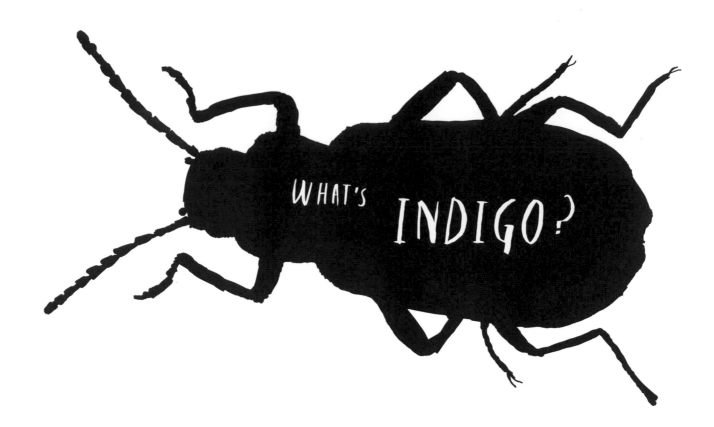

WHAT'S INDIGO?

For Mary

WHAT'S VIOLET?

First published in America 2021
by Berbay Publishing Pty Ltd
PO Box 133
Kew East
Victoria 3102 Australia
www.berbaybooks.com

Text and Illustrations © John Canty 2020

The moral right of the author
and illustrator has been asserted.

Publisher: Alexandra Yatomi-Clarke
Designed by John Canty
Edited by Nancy Conescu

Cataloguing-in-publication entry is available
from the National Library of Australia.
http://catalogue.nla.gov.au

Printed in China through Asia Pacific Offset

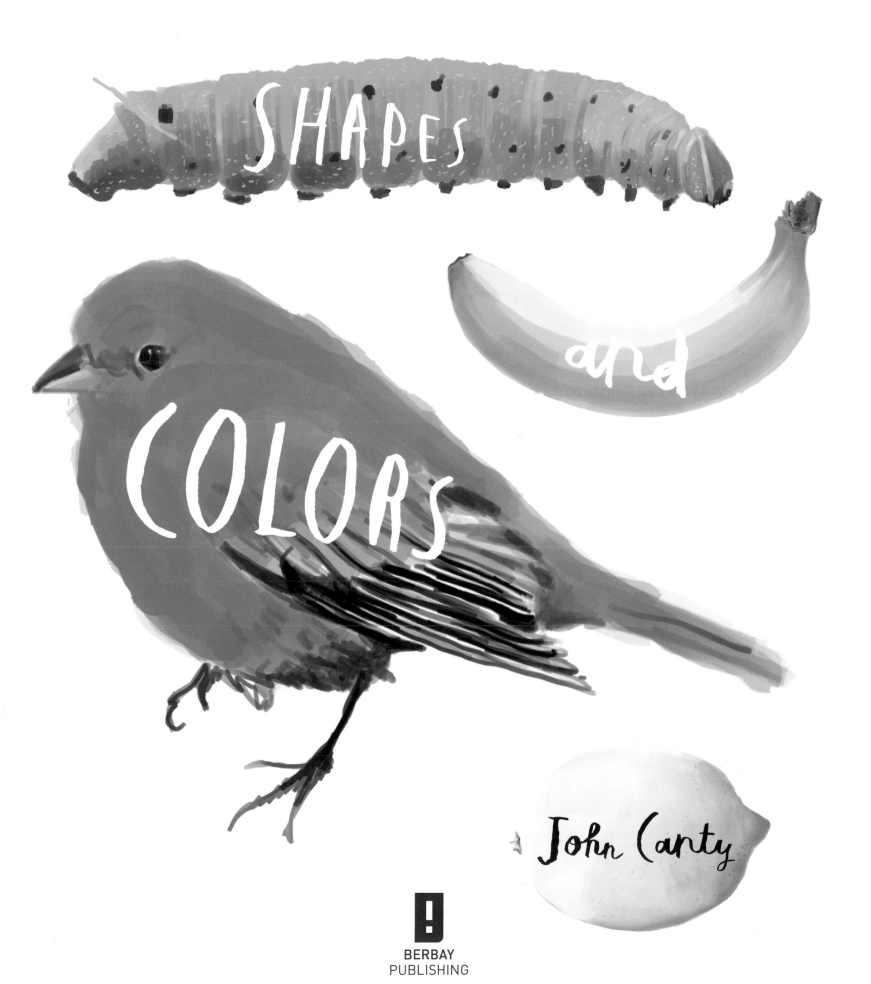

Shapes and Colors

COLORS

and

John Canty

BERBAY
PUBLISHING

BALLOON   RIBBON

FIRE TRUCK

STRAWBERRY

CHERRIES

TOMATO

ROSE

LADYBUG

WHAT'S
ORA

NGE?

POPSICLE

ORANGE

GOLDFISH

SAFETY VEST

AUTUMN
LEAF

PUMPKIN

TRAFFIC CONE

CARROT

WHAT'S
YELL

WHAT'S GR

LEAVES

CATERPILLAR

FROG

APPLE

LIZARD

TREE

PEAS

GRASSHOPPER

WHAT'S BL

BOOTS

BUTTERFLY

WHALE

BLUEBEARIES

BLUEBIRD

SPADE

BUCKET

JEANS

WHAT'S IN

KNIFE

BEETLE

CAP

SNAKE

SPOON

FORK

T-SHIRT

CRAYON

WHAT'S VI

CUP

COMB

SEA STAR

GRAPES

SHORTS

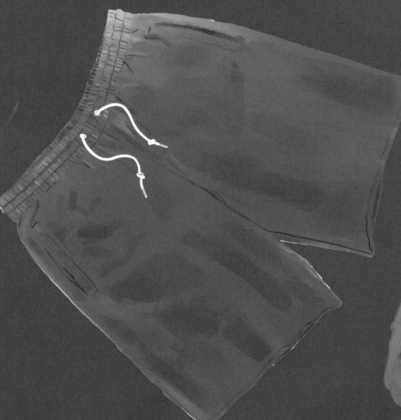

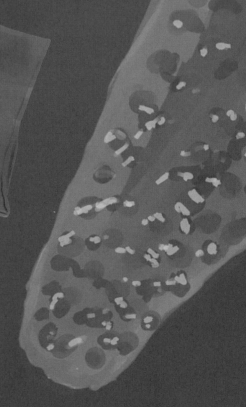

SUNGLASSES

SCISSORS

VIOLETS

WHAT COLORS CAN WE FIND IN THE CITY?

WHAT COLORS CAN WE FIND IN THE COUNTRY?

ALL THE COLORS
OF OUR WORLD.

RED

YELLOW

BLUE

VIOLET